Little Grey Rabbit

Fuzzypeg Goes to School

Little Grey Rabbit

FUZZYPEG GOES TO SCHOOL

By Alison Uttley
Pictures by Margaret Tempest

templar
books

It was bedtime, and Fuzzypeg the little Hedgehog sat eating his bread and milk.

"Can I have a tale tonight?" he asked.

Old Hedgehog scratched his head trying to think of a tale. Then he sang a song instead. "I learned that in my schooldays," he said.

"Can I go to
school one day?"
asked Fuzzypeg.
"You can go
tomorrow if you're
ready on time,"
said Mrs Hedgehog.

Fuzzypeg hopped
around the room for
joy, then he hopped
up to bed and called
goodnight to the moon.

The next morning
Fuzzypeg awoke early.

"I'm going to school
today," he sang and
rolled downstairs in a
prickly ball.

Old Hedgehog had a
neat parcel under his arm.

"It's a schoolbag for
you," he said. "Grey
Rabbit gave it to me
when she heard you
were going to school."

It had a big pocket for sandwiches, two little pockets for books and a tiny one for the penny to pay the teacher. Fuzzypeg put it on at once and started off for school.

"Don't be late," called his mother.

As Fuzzypeg went down the lane he saw his cousins.

"I'm going to school," said Fuzzypeg proudly.

"We'll come too!" said the little hedgehogs.

"Quick, or we'll be late," called Fuzzypeg.

They trotted along the lane when Hare came lolloping along in his bright blue coat.

"Hello," he said. "What's in your bag?"

"Sandwiches," said Fuzzypeg, handing them out.

"Now you have room for other things," said Hare. So they filled the bag with bindweed, forget-me-nots and foxgloves.

"That's all for today," said Hare, running off, for he had seen Grey Rabbit coming towards them.

Grey Rabbit was astonished to see the little hedgehogs sitting on the grass.

"What are you doing?" she asked. "Run to school as fast as you can or your teacher will be cross."

So off they ran under the gate and across the meadow to where Jonathan Rabbit had his school.

In the distance a little hare stood in a grove of bluebells, shaking them.

"That's the school bell," said a thrush. "You'll be late."

The three hedgehogs raced to the school door, pushed aside a leafy curtain and entered the schoolroom.

"Remember school begins at nine o'clock and don't be late," said the teacher.

They sat down next to the other little animals, then the teacher asked them all some questions.

"Which flower helps us to remember?" he asked.

Fuzzypeg drew the forget-me-nots from his bag. "Quite right," said the teacher. "Now which flower shuts its eyes when it rains?"

Fuzzypeg held up the white bindweed.

"Right again! And which flower makes gloves for cold paws?"

Every animal knew and shouted "Foxgloves!" before Fuzzypeg could get the foxglove from his satchel.

Just then, Fuzzypeg saw Little Grey Rabbit
coming towards them. All the animals rushed
to meet her, and begged her for a story.

She sat in the shade of a tree and started
a tale, but had only just begun when there
was a terrible roaring noise.

"Woof! Woof! Woof!"

Everyone shrieked and ran helter-skelter up and down the field.

But Grey Rabbit stood very still for she thought she recognized the voice.

"Come out, Hare," she said sternly. "You can't deceive me."

All the little animals came creeping out.
Then out of the stream crawled a very
bedraggled little hedgehog.

"Poor Fuzzypeg," said Grey Rabbit.
"You'd better go straight home to bed."

"I don't want to go home, I've only just begun," said Fuzzypeg in a quavering voice.

But Grey Rabbit took him by the hand and hurried him home.

Fuzzypeg was popped into bed with a bowl of soup and cup of tea. Grey Rabbit sang at his bedside while he sneezed.

"What did you learn besides swimming?"
asked Old Hedgehog, when he came home
at last. But by then Fuzzypeg was almost
asleep, quite tired out from all his learning.

THE END

A TEMPLAR BOOK

This edition first published in the UK in 2018 by Templar Publishing,
an imprint of Kings Road Publishing, part of the Bonnier Publishing Group,
The Plaza, 535 King's Road, London, SW10 0SZ
www.templarco.co.uk
www.bonnierpublishing.com

Original edition first published in the UK in 1938
by William Collins Sons & Co Ltd

Text copyright © 2018 by The Alison Uttley Literary Property Trust
Illustration copyright © 2018 by The Estate of Margaret Tempest
Design copyright © 2018 by Kings Road Publishing Limited

This edition edited by Susan Dickinson and Ruth Symons
Additional design by Nathalie Eyraud and Adam Allori

3 5 7 9 10 8 6 4 2

All rights reserved

ISBN 978-1-78741-229-3

Printed in China